SIMON
STEPS INTO THE RING

To all the women who encouraged me to see this project through.
To Steve, the man of my life, who lovingly accepts all of my emotions.
—M.M.

Library and Archives Canada Cataloguing in Publication

Title: Simon steps into the ring / Marylène Monette ; illustrated by Marion Arbona ; translated by Sophie B. Watson.
Other titles: Combats de Ti-Coeur. English
Names: Monette, Marylène, 1978– author. | Arbona, Marion, illustrator. | Watson, Sophie B., translator.
Description: Translation of: Les combats de Ti-Coeur.

Identifiers: Canadiana 20190170697 | ISBN 9781459821811 (hardcover)
Classification: LCC PS8626.O535 C6513 2020 | DDC jC843/.6—dc23

Library of Congress Control Number: 2019943988
Simultaneously published in Canada and the United States in 2020

Summary: A little boy learns to acknowledge his temper in this illustrated picture book for young readers.

*Orca Book Publishers is committed to reducing the consumption of nonrenewable resources in the making
of our books. We make every effort to use materials that support a sustainable future.*

Orca Book Publishers gratefully acknowledges the support for its publishing programs provided by
the following agencies: the Government of Canada, the Canada Council for the Arts and the Province
of British Columbia through the BC Arts Council and the Book Publishing Tax Credit.

We acknowledge the financial support of the Government of Canada through the National
Translation Program for Book Publishing, an initiative of the *Roadmap for Canada's Official
Languages 2013-2018: Education, Immigration, Communities,* for our translation activities.

The illustrations in *Simon Steps into the Ring* were drawn with gouache, pencil and charcoal. I wanted to use a rather limited
color palette, where notes of red and bright pink dominate and symbolize both fierceness and love. —Marion Arbona
Cover and interior artwork by Marion Arbona
Translated by Sophie B. Watson

ORCA BOOK PUBLISHERS
orcabook.com

Printed and bound in South Korea.

23 22 21 20 • 4 3 2 1

SIMON
STEPS INTO THE RING

MARYLÈNE MONETTE
ILLUSTRATED BY MARION ARBONA
TRANSLATED BY SOPHIE B. WATSON

ORCA BOOK PUBLISHERS

My guts are like a bowl of spaghetti, tangled up and full of knots. My heart is playing a drum solo. I have suffered in the hallway for half an hour.

Everyone stares. I am the condemned one.

CLICKETY! CLACKETY! CLICKETY!

Mom arrives, her high heels clickety-clacketing angrily.
We'll be spending a nasty quarter of an hour in the principal's office.
In a few moments she'll learn that her Simon has been a terror.

I'm not always the same me. That's the problem.
Uncle Richard, who has lived with us since Dad left, says it's
as if I have puppets inside me playing different characters.
It's like these puppets take turns inside the ring. They dive
headlong into a boxing match before I can stop them.

DING! DING!

In the green corner, **Simon the Fearful** awaits his sentence.

In the blue corner sits **Simon the Arrogant**, who got worked up an hour ago in class. He is sure of himself—square shoulders, glaring eyes and big mouth. He is a kid who attacks anyone who annoys him, hurling insults like roundhouse kicks.

In my frenzy, I mistook Mr. Louis, my teacher, for another boxer. I should never have spoken to him the way I did. I used words I'm not allowed to say. Bad decision. This whole day has been round after round, fight after fight.

In the yellow corner, meet the first contestant of the day, **Simon the Perfect Brother**, the one all little sisters dream of. I take my sweet sister by the hand and—hop!—off to school we go.

The neighbor's dog, Max, barks after us. He wants out. "I feel as trapped as Max," my sister confides. "Valerie won't let me play with Leah or anyone else. She says I can only be friends with her."

"If Valerie really liked you, she wouldn't stop you from playing with other people," Simon the Perfect Brother says. "You're free! Don't let yourself be pushed around."

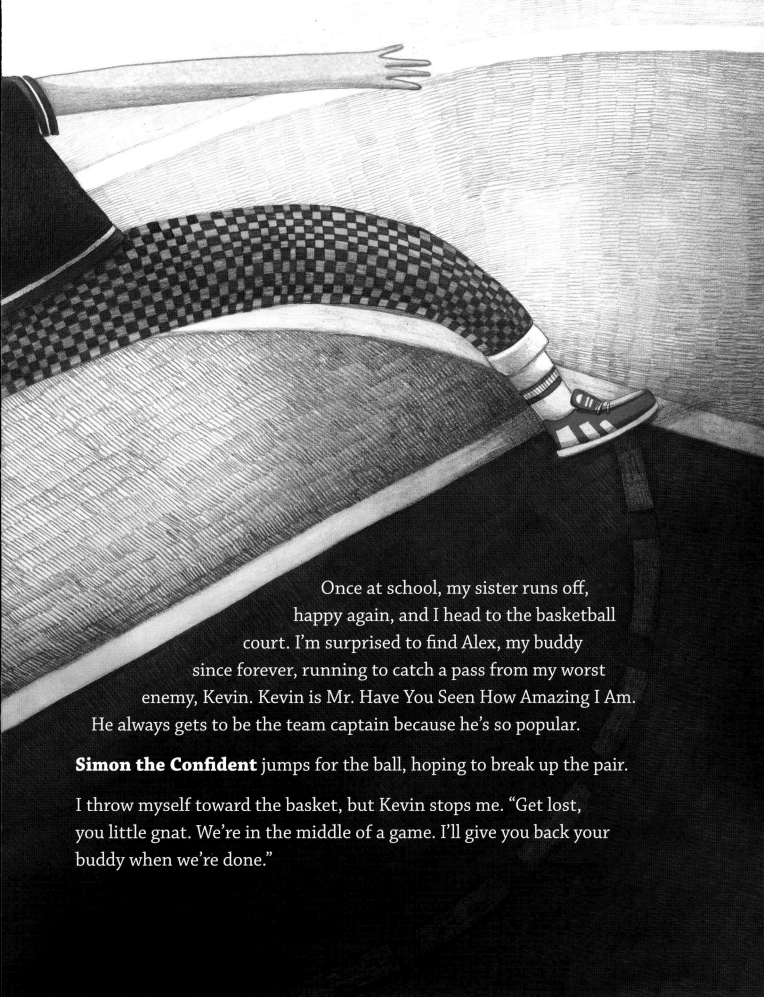

Once at school, my sister runs off,
happy again, and I head to the basketball
court. I'm surprised to find Alex, my buddy
since forever, running to catch a pass from my worst
enemy, Kevin. Kevin is Mr. Have You Seen How Amazing I Am.
He always gets to be the team captain because he's so popular.

Simon the Confident jumps for the ball, hoping to break up the pair.

I throw myself toward the basket, but Kevin stops me. "Get lost,
you little gnat. We're in the middle of a game. I'll give you back your
buddy when we're done."

DING! DING!

Simon the Confident can't think of an answer. He turns into **Simon the Frozen**, hangs up his gloves and complains to Madame Lucie.

DING! DING!

Luckily, the next contestant in the ring is **Simon the Good Student**. He tries his best in art class. His eyes sparkle, and he has lots of energy. He refuses to make even the smallest mistake with his pencil. He spends the whole class making his comic strip as good as it can be.

I like this me. He's a real hero when he shows up.

DING! DING!

But my hero doesn't show up after lunch.

I enter the classroom. Mr. Louis is sticking animal posters on the wall. It smells like science. Yes! My heart beats happily. **Simon the Joyous** is here. He is the lightweight champion of science!

"Today, friends, we'll start with group work on animal families," Mr. Louis says. "Each team will study one animal family."

I'm an animal fanatic! This is the project of the year. Alex will be my research partner, and we'll choose reptiles...

"I have already divided everyone into groups," Mr. Louis adds.

DING! DING!

No! We can't choose who we want in our group! I have to work with quiet Amélie and *Kevin*! To top it off, Amélie picks fish. *Fish!* The universe is against me.

Simon the Grumpy steps into the ring to defend his title.

DING! DING!

Simon the Lazy joins forces with **Simon the Grumpy**. His hands go limp. He clenches his jaw. His eyes half close.

I slouch in my chair. I have no intention whatsoever of working.

"Hey, Shrimp. Got any ideas?"

"I have zero ideas. It's a stupid topic."

"The only thing that's stupid here is you."

Simon the Arrogant can't help but jump into the ring. He fights back. He shouts rude words.

"Okay, guys, what's happening here?" Mr. Louis asks.

"You! You did it on purpose, putting me with him!
You've never liked me anyway.
Your assignment is useless! You can stuff..."

The round is over.
Mr. Louis sends me to the principal's office.
It's a knockout blow.

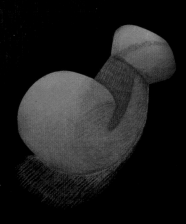

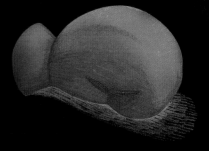

CLICKETY! CLACKETY! CLICKETY!

Mom is taking me home. The principal has suspended me from school until tomorrow. Mom scolds me sternly and points at me accusingly, like an angry referee. She tells me my room is my prison until further notice.

Other consequences are no video games for a month and extra homework, and I have to write apology letters to Mr. Louis and my study group.

DING! DING!

The worst consequence shows up just then.

I hear Uncle Richard's footsteps.

I promised him I'd be careful, and I haven't kept my promise.

I know I've disappointed him.

The door squeaks. **Simon the Ashamed** comes on the scene. He fixes his wet eyes on the floor. His cheeks are on fire, his shoulders hunched.

"Hard day, Simon?"

Strangely, Uncle Richard doesn't look mad. He looks understanding!

"I lost control again. I can't stop myself."

"Are you ashamed of yourself because you didn't choose the good you?"

I nod yes through my tears.

"Tell me all about it, Simon. It'll do you some good."

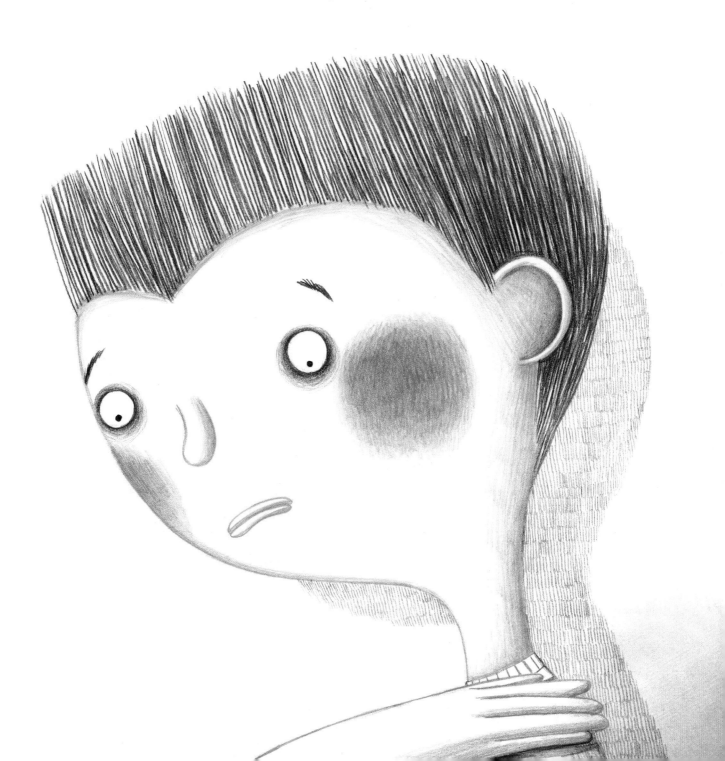

I tell Uncle Richard every detail of the problems I had all day.

"You know, I think all the Simons can be useful," he says. "But at the right time."

"Who decides which one should be in charge?"

"The little referee inside you. The referee must judge the situation and make the right decision."

"That won't be easy in my case."

"Don't get discouraged. I'll give you some tricks. You've already improved. You didn't let violence burst from your arms. That's a good first step. You need to be proud of yourself for that."

DING! DING!

Simon the Confident straightens his shoulders.
He moves slowly but surely toward the ring...

Which me will I present to the world next?

DO YOU HAVE LOTS OF "ME'S"? TRY THE FOLLOWING ACTIVITIES TO GET TO KNOW YOURSELF BETTER. OR FIND SOMEONE WHO IS IMPORTANT TO YOU AND DO THEM TOGETHER.

Look at the characters shown four pages back, opposite the referee. According to you, which "me" does each character represent?

Are you like any of them sometimes?

DING! DING!

Name or draw six little boxers inside you.

Do they show up in the house?
At school? When you're with your friends?

Which ones do you prefer?
Which are more difficult to manage?

DING! DING!

Choose two "me's" who are fighting inside you.

Describe the kind of situation that winds them up.

What are the strengths and weaknesses of each "me"?

Find an image, an accessory or an animal to represent them.

DING! DING!

If you're in the mood, draw the "me's" in the boxing ring or make puppets to represent them.

In your drawings or with your puppets, make them talk to each other. You could also create a skit.

Some of these activities were created by Mélanie Filion and Richard Robillard.